CARTOON NETWORK BOOKS
Penguin Young Readers Group
An Imprint of Penguin Random House LLC

TM and © Cartoon Network. (s17). All rights reserved. Published in 2017 by Cartoon Network Books, an imprint of Penguin Random House LLC, 345 Hudson Street, New York, New York 10014. Manufactured in China.

ISBN 9780515158021

10 9 8 7 6 5 4 3 2 1

ADVENTURE TIME

Friendship
and Junk

illustrated by JJ Harrison

CARTOON NETWORK BOOKS

An Imprint of Penguin Random House

Friends are . . . .

. . . bros!

... trust pounds!

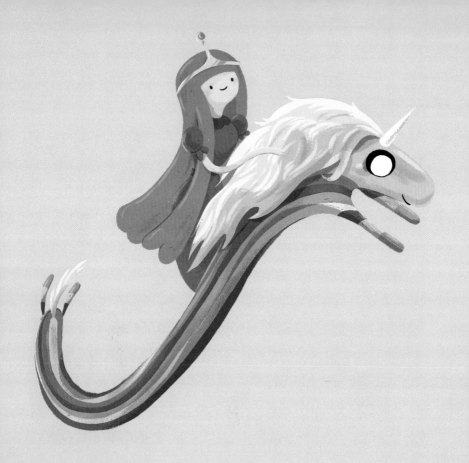

. . . adventurers
for life!

. . . playing video games!

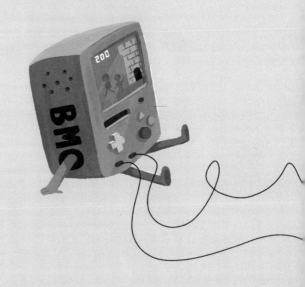

. . . dancing if they want to dance!

. . . real with
each other!

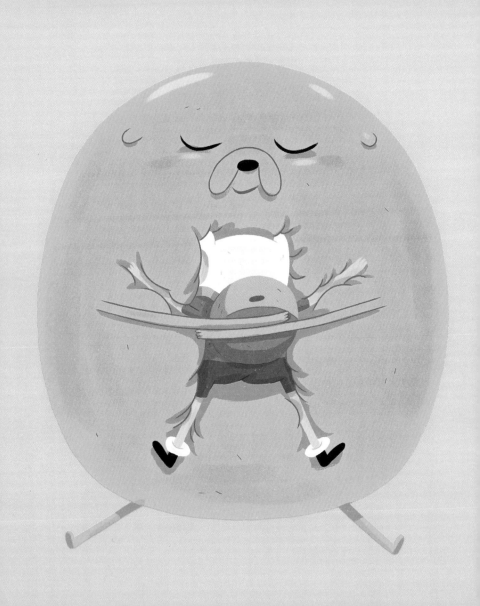

. . . hugging it out!

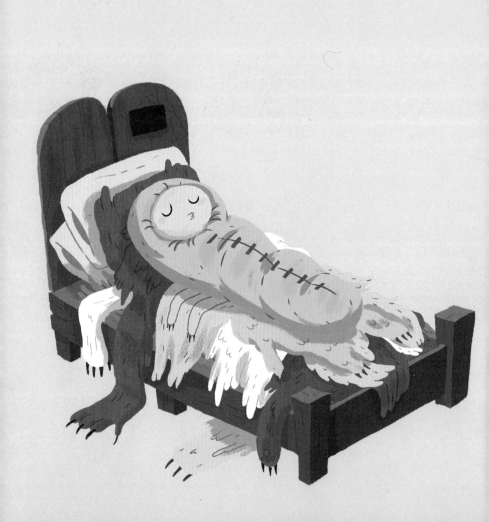

. . . forever!

That's why . . .

. . . you never mess
with *friends!*